WITHDRAWN

THE
CELESTIAL RIVER

THE
CELESTIAL RIVER

CREATION TALES OF THE MILKY WAY

ANDREA STENN STRYER

August House Publishers, Inc.
LITTLE ROCK

ARL-BOG
BOGART BRANCH LIBRARY
C/O ATHENS REGIONAL LIBRARY
2025 BAXTER STREET/ATHENS
ATL

ATHENS REGIONAL LIBRARY
2025 BAXTER STREET
ATHENS, GA 30606

© 1998 by Andrea Stenn Stryer.
All rights reserved. This book, or parts thereof,
may not be reproduced, or publicly presented,
in any form without permission.
Published 1998 by August House, Inc.,
P.O. Box 3223, Little Rock, Arkansas, 72203,
501-372-5450.

Printed in the United States of America

10 9 8 7 6 5 4 3 2 1

LIBRARY OF CONGRESS CATALOGING-IN-PUBLICATION DATA

Stryer, Andrea Stenn, 1938-
The celestial river : creation tales of the
Milky Way / Andrea Stenn Stryer.
p.   cm.
Includes bibliographical references.
ISBN 0-87483-529-1 (hardcover). —ISBN 0-87483-528-3 (pbk.)
1. Milky Way—Folklore. 2. Tales. 3. Mythology. I. Title.
GR625.S77   1998
398.26—DC21   98-26813

Executive editor: Liz Parkhurst
Project editor: Jason H. Maynard
Cover design: Wendell E. Hall
Interior drawings: Wendell E. Hall
Book design: Shirley Brainard

AUGUST HOUSE, INC.   PUBLISHERS   LITTLE ROCK

In remembrance of my dad, Frederick Stenn,
who made the gods and heroes
of the heavens come alive.

Contents

Introduction

The Milky Way Galaxy is the large spiral galaxy in which our solar system lies. This rapidly spinning disk of stars is made up of hundreds of billions of stars—all of them our near neighbors. The broad band of light stretching across our night sky is only a small part of the galaxy, just a slice of the whole disk.

Long ago, before the lights of cities dimmed our view of the heavens, anyone who looked up on a clear night could see the Milky Way. The glowing ribbon of light seemed almost close enough to touch. It reminded ancient people of common things around them: a river, a road, milk, or strewn wheat. But they gave the luminous stream vivid names, such as Celestial River, Star-Filled Basket, and Path to the Place of Abundance.

With these names came remarkable stories of how the Milky Way was formed—stories that grew from each culture's fears, needs, and hopes. In each story, one central character actually creates the Milky Way. Although the creator may be a person, a god or goddess, or even an animal, the motives are always driven by a strong passion. Each tale is a unique explanation of how the Milky Way came to arch across the skies.

THE SEVENTH NIGHT OF THE SEVENTH MOON

∽

ANCIENT JAPAN

This legend originated in China, where the Milky Way is called Tien Ho, Celestial River. In the seventh century, the tale crossed the East China Sea to nearby Japan.

In old Japan, each year, on the seventh night of the seventh moon, the people celebrated the festival of Tanabata-Sama, the Weaving Lady of the Milky Way. They cut a fresh, green stalk of bamboo and placed it on the roof or in the garden. To this pole, they attached strips of colored paper with poems about the weaver. At the festival's end, they cast the bamboo into a stream and watched it float away.

Two groups of stars, in addition to the Milky Way, were highlights of the festival. One was the herdsman—three stars in a row suggesting a man leading an ox. It can be found on the west side of the Milky Way in the constellation called Lyra. Opposite, on the eastern side, is the weaver—three stars suggesting a woman at her loom, in the constellation called Aquila.

The seventh month falls in August, when the Perseid meteor showers flash across the sky. In old Japan, some saw these meteors not as shooting stars but as magpies flying to form a bridge across the Celestial River.

∽

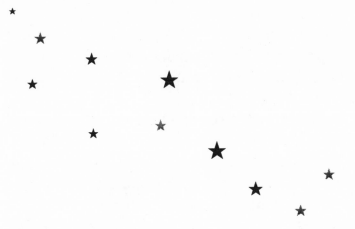

The huge vault of the heavens was ruled by the divine power, Kami. This great god and careful ruler kept close watch over his subjects to make sure that all did their jobs well.

Now Kami had a very beautiful daughter by the name of Tanabata. She was by far the most talented weaver in the heavens. Only she could make cloth worthy of her honorable father.

As the sun's first rays lit the heavenly vault each day, Tanabata opened the door of their dwelling and sat at her loom with the finest spun yarn. While the sun crossed the sky, she passed the shuttle through the warp, back and forth, back and forth. And with the rhythm came poetry. By the time the sun had sunk beneath the western horizon each day, she had created a new poem for herself and had woven another lovely length of cloth for her father.

Nothing took her from her beloved work until the morning when Tanabata looked up from her loom. A handsome herdsman was driving his oxen past the gate.

Tanabata rose from the loom and went to the doorway. The herdsman had stopped to look at the dwelling. He smiled when he saw the young woman. Lowering her eyes, Tanabata blushed.

"Oftimes have I passed behind your home where glorious robes are airing," said the herdsman. "Are you the weaver of such fine cloth?"

With eyes still downcast, Tanabata nodded.

"I am Hikoboshi," the herdsman said. "What is your name, fair one?"

The moment Tanabata lifted her head and spoke her name, she knew that her heart belonged to Hikoboshi.

"Lovely Tanabata, come. Walk with me to the meadow where my oxen graze."

The maiden gladly joined the herdsman. They followed the oxen to the meadow. There, Hikoboshi showed Tanabata baby rabbits nesting under a bush and tiny field mice scampering in the grass. He took a small flute from his belt and played sweet airs while Tanabata gathered wildflowers. From these, she wove a circlet for the herdsman's belt. Handing it to him, she whispered a new poem inspired by the blooming meadow.

When evening came, the two, holding hands,

slowly followed the oxen to Tanabata's home.

As the great Kami entered the house that night, Tanabata said, "August father, it is my deepest wish to marry Hikoboshi, the herdsman."

Seeing how overcome with love she was, the god answered, "Daughter, it shall be so. Your marriage will have my blessing."

Soon the two were wed. They moved to a small cottage nearby with their possessions. Tanabata's loom sat in the main room, awaiting the weaver's touch. The oxen grazed in the adjoining field awaiting the herdsman's lead.

The couple joyfully spent all their time together. During the day, they would stroll through the meadows until they found a cool bamboo forest. There, Hikoboshi played gentle flute melodies for his bride. When the last echo died away, Tanabata recited poems, poems of love.

As twilight lengthened the shadows, they would slowly wander home. There, they fed each other delicacies and watched the glowing coals in the grate.

Alas, in their joy, Tanabata and Hikoboshi forgot their tasks. The loom sat silent, motes of dust falling on it. The neglected oxen broke through the wall and wandered over the fields of heaven.

All the while, the great Kami watched the couple's heedlessness, becoming more and more angry. Finally, in his fury, he thundered, "You two have disregarded the duties that are yours. As punishment, you shall be separated—for eternity!"

Kami, with his mighty arm, opened the heavenly floodgate. The waters burst forth between the two lovers. "This celestial river will part you forever."

The stream coursed, separating the two banks more and more. As the waters spread, Tanabata watched Hikoboshi recede farther and farther away on the opposite bank. When she could behold him no longer, she fell to the ground, deep sobs wracking her body.

A day passed. Tanabata forced herself to get up and return to the loom. She began to weave, but tears filled her eyes, blurring her sight. When her father came, he saw that she had woven only a drab strip, drenched with tears.

Tanabata looked up at him. "August father, I deserve punishment. I should have been at my loom, but I was not. I should have woven glorious fabric for you, but I did not. I will do as you bid, but I beseech you, have mercy. If I am to weave well, I must know that I will see Hikoboshi again. Give us some hope of seeing one another, if only for a brief time."

The great Kami saw how desolate she was. He took pity on the lovers.

"I will make this exception," the god said. "Once a year, on the seventh night of the seventh moon, you may briefly see one another. But the night must be cloudless. Then will I send a thousand magpies to form a bridge over the river for you to cross."

And so it has been ever since. On the seventh night of the seventh moon each year, when it is cloudless, the two eagerly make their way to the bridge. They step joyously from wing to wing, hands outstretched to hasten their meeting.

But if it is cloudy on that night, no birds appear to bridge the Celestial River. Tanabata and Hikoboshi stand on either side of the stormy waters, unable to catch even a glimpse of their beloved.

During the long year, the separated couple work hard, fulfilling their duties. When the hint of autumn chills the summer air, Tanabata and Hikoboshi begin to watch the sky. If their special night is clear, the wings of the birds will touch, tip to tip, and arch up over the Celestial River. As soon as the bridge is formed, the two will reach out to one another, grateful for the seventh night of the seventh moon.

The Milk That Flew Across the Sky

∾

Ancient Greece

The ancient Greeks saw the Milky Way as a gigantic spill of milk. It looked as if an invisible pitcher had tipped, pouring milk into a sometimes broad, sometimes narrow stream, with tongues of milk branching off into the sky.

The Greeks called this broad band of misty light galaxias kyklos. It means Milky Circle, from which we get the name Milky Way.

In Greek mythology, the Olympian gods always served as central characters in the various plots. They also played major roles in the tales of the creation of the Milky Way. These gods and goddesses were an unruly lot. Zeus, the supreme god, was always looking for dazzling women, whether goddess or mortal. His wife, Hera, queen of the heavens, was deeply jealous—and with good reason. Whenever she discovered that Zeus had made a new conquest, her fury had no bounds.

Most feats were simple for Zeus, but the one thing he could not do was to make a human immortal. Therein lies the tale.

∾

The great god Zeus rose from his heavenly throne, ready to embark on a new adventure—an adventure of love. Down he came from Mount Olympus, crossing valleys and meadows, rivers and lakes. Near Thebes, he paused on the banks of a cool stream. There he caught sight of a young woman, still damp from her bath, combing her long tresses. The sunlight danced on her dark wavy hair. Plucking a scarlet poppy, she glanced around. The god saw her wide brown eyes and curved brows, her smooth skin and slender neck.

Zeus recognized the maiden as the lovely Alcmene. *Not only is she beautiful,* he thought, *but she is also from a family of heroes. She is the grand-daughter of Perseus, who slew the terrible Medusa.*

At once, Zeus knew that he wanted to have a child with Alcmene. A mighty god such as he should have an equally brave, strong son, one powerful enough to do his bidding, one daring enough to carry out incredible deeds. Zeus was certain that if he had a son with this mortal woman, the child would inherit strength and courage—not only from Zeus, but also from Perseus's family—making a great hero.

Zeus took another long look at Alcmene. Nothing would do until she became his latest conquest. He began making his plans.

As it happened, this virtuous young woman had just married the ruler of Thebes, King Amphitryon. Alcmene had agreed to be his queen, provided he avenge the death of her eight brothers, whom she mourned. Amphitryon willingly accepted this task. Immediately after the wedding, he left to do battle with her enemy.

While the king was still away, Zeus disguised himself as the returning King Amphitryon. He regaled Alcmene with all the details of the successful battle, and Alcmene was deeply pleased with her husband's deeds and prowess. It never entered her mind to doubt who this man was. In order to spend more time making love, Zeus stopped the sun from rising for three earthly nights. Therefore, Alcmene thought that only one night had passed.

The following day when her true husband, Amphitryon, returned home, he started to tell Alcmene about the battle. She stared at him.

"Why are you telling me again?" she asked. "Don't you remember? You told me all about it last night."

King Amphitryon gasped. "How could I have told you? Only at this very hour have I passed through the gates of Thebes. Only I have this knowledge. I was not the one who spoke of the battle. Who could have described to you what I alone know?"

No sooner had he finished speaking than the couple realized that only Zeus could have been aware of the battle. Only Zeus could have been so audacious. Both Alcmene and the real King Amphitryon were horror-struck. Unless they could appease Zeus's wife, Hera, her wrath would surely strike them.

Alcmene, now pregnant, was frantic with fear for her unborn child, her husband, and herself. To save the House of Amphitryon, she knew she would have to abandon her baby in the country-side where it would be exposed to the winds and wild animals.

Nine months later, Alcmene went into labor. The baby was born and the nurse, after washing him, brought him to his mother. Alcmene called him Iphicles, carefully placing her hand under his head. Like all infants, he wasn't strong enough to hold up his head.

Just as she gave Iphicles back to the nurse, labor pains began anew. A second son was born. Alcmene was immediately struck by his eyes, which blazed radiantly. To her great surprise, this child lifted his head from her supporting hold, grabbed onto her finger, and pulled himself up. *Such incredible strength,* she thought. *This younger twin must be Zeus's son. I shall call him Heracles.*

But Alcmene had to act swiftly, for the cloud of Hera's jealousy hung heavy over her. Though exhausted, she rose from the birthing bed and wrapped Heracles, Zeus's newborn son, in a woolen cloak. Clutching the bundle, Alcmene stole through the gates of Thebes.

Once outside the walls of the city, she ran into the fields beyond, passing gnarled olive trees and tripping across the scattered stones. Alcmene hollowed out a small niche under a bush. Stifling a sob, she put the baby down and left him to his fate. She turned and disappeared back into the city as quickly as she'd come.

From Mount Olympus, Zeus saw all this. He knew that he must act swiftly to save his son. Above all, he had to find a way of making Heracles immortal.

The problem was that the only way for a human to become immortal was to drink some of Hera's milk. Zeus knew that Hera would never willingly give that child her milk. The greatest of gods would have to trick Hera into feeding Heracles.

Zeus spoke to his daughter, Athena. "Of all those on Mount Olympus, you most clearly understand what I am feeling and thinking."

The goddess of wisdom smiled. "How could I not?"

Zeus looked fondly at his daughter. "Now I must have your advice." And he proceeded to tell her exactly what he wanted. After some thought, the goddess devised a clever scheme.

She took Hera walking in the stony field outside of Thebes. As they strolled amidst the wind–blown poppies, Athena pretended to discover an abandoned infant.

"Hera, come! Look what I've found. Such a sturdy, active boy. How could his mother have given him up? She must have lost her wits, poor thing, to have left him here. You have milk, Hera. Give this poor little fellow some sustenance."

Without thinking, Hera picked up the baby. As soon as she put him to her breast, Heracles starting sucking voraciously. Hera let out a scream of pain. As she pulled him away, her milk shot up, reaching high and far into the sky. She flung the baby away and fled from the field.

Athena hastened over and picked up the unharmed infant. Cradling him in one arm, she passed through the gates of Thebes and into the city. Handing young Heracles to his mother, Athena said, "Guard this child and raise him well, Alcmene. He is destined to carry out great feats for mortals and mighty deeds for the gods."

And so it was that Hera's milk, which gave

immortality to Heracles, also spread across the sky. The droplets of milk, white against the dark of night, radiated from horizon to horizon and became the Milky Way.

YIKÁÍSDÁHÍ, WHICH AWAITS THE DAWN

◇

NAVAJO

The Navajo people live in the Four Corners area of the United States, where the states of Colorado, New Mexico, Utah, and Arizona meet. They call themselves Diné and live in family groups that are scattered about the vast reservation. An important part of their way of life is raising sheep for food and wool. The traditional Navajo lives in a hogan, a small five-, six-, or eight-sided home built of poles and clay. There they dye, spin, and weave the wool. They cook meals in the center of the hogan, under the smoke-hole. The family sleeps near the fire, sharing the space with orphan lambs. When the sun's last rays vanish from the sky, the family gathers around the fire to keep warm and share stories.

The Navajo value order in their lives; order guides all behavior and brings beauty, harmony, and blessedness. Because the stars, over time, are constant, they remind the people of the importance of maintaining harmony.

In Navajo tales, Coyote, the trickster, has no regard for order. Harmony means nothing to him, for he is restless and untameable.

◇

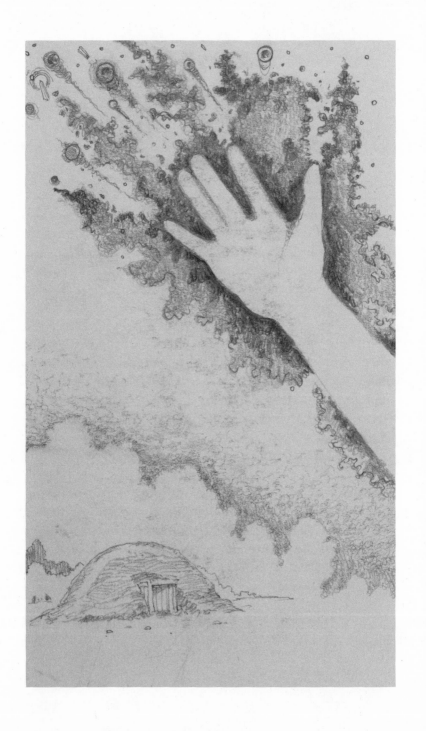

It was the Beginning Time. The creation gods required a gathering place. It was the time to discuss the world-to-be and what they should create for it. They would need a hogan, a winter home, for this crucial meeting.

The hogan's frame, the gods said, must have the poles placed in each of the cardinal directions. At once, they commanded the first two poles to be the door frame and to place themselves on the east, so that the first rays of the rising sun would shine into the door. Then, just as the sun moves across the sky, the next pole was ordered to set itself on the south, then the west, and last of all the north pole, to hold all the others in place.

The gods covered the poles with sunbeams and rainbows, and made rooms of turquoise and ladders of white shell. They sang the blessing song, and lastly, to bring peace and plenty, they put a pinch of cornmeal on each of the four main beams.

The hogan was now ready for the all-important gathering. The gods arrived one by one and sat around the center fire, with the smokehole above it. Coyote slinked in and curled up along one side. The last god to arrive was Hastyésini, the Fire God. All the other gods' eyes were on him. He sat down, not saying a thing.

Hastyésini lifted his ankle, on which he wore a shiny circlet of stars called Dilyehe. Then Hastyésini stamped his foot four times, once for the east, once for the south, once for the west, and once for the north. At the first stamp, Dilyehe jumped to his knee, on the second to his hip, on the third to his shoulder, and at the fourth stamp Dilyehe landed on his left temple.

"Ah," the gods sighed, "that is so beautiful. Hastyésini, you must fill the night sky with those exquisite crystals of light."

Hastyésini pulled from his garments a pouch made of the softest deerskin. He reached into the pouch and scrutinized each crystal to choose the perfect ones, those that sparkled in the firelight. First, he selected and placed in the sky North Fire, the star that never moves, the faithful guide of the traveller at night. Then he laid out several brilliant crystals in patterns—or constellations, as he called them. He laid out Whirling Male and Whirling Female in the north. He put Man with Feet Spread Apart in the east; First Big One and Rabbit Tracks in the south; and Horned Rattler, Bear, and Thunder in the west.

After placing even more constellations in the heavens, he made a copy of Dilyehe, the star cluster from his left temple, and placed it on high.

All this time, Coyote watched impatiently. He had had enough of Hastyésini's slow pace. All of this was taking far too long. He thumped his tail on the ground, scratched his belly, tapped his feet, and yawned. Hastyésini had just dug his hand into the small sack and pulled out another large handful of crystals when Coyote grabbed the deerskin pouch.

Coyote shook out the last of the crystals. He scattered them in all four directions hither and thither. They fell in no pattern whatsoever, which is why so many stars do not belong to a constellation.

"At least they're all up there and we don't have to wait for that snail of a god to place and name each star," Coyote sneered.

But Hastyésini had the last word. He still had a large handful of crystals.

With great care, Hastyésini dispersed them completely across the middle of the sky. "All of these—this stretch of crystals together—make Yikáísdáhí, Which Awaits the Dawn," he said.

Then, just as attentively, Hastyésini took a glowing ember from the fire. He held it up to North Fire. That instant, the crystal was ignited. It twinkled brightly in the dark night. Like a lamp-lighter, he did the same with each of the other constellations.

Finally, Hastyésini plucked one more coal, of the deepest crimson, out of the fire. Starting at the near horizon, he drew this ember up overhead, and then down to the far horizon, lighting the sweep of crystals that crossed the sky.

Hastyésini sat back and gazed upward. He had completed the night sky, for now Yikáísdáhí was glowing, that stretch of stars, the Milky Way, Which Awaits the Dawn.

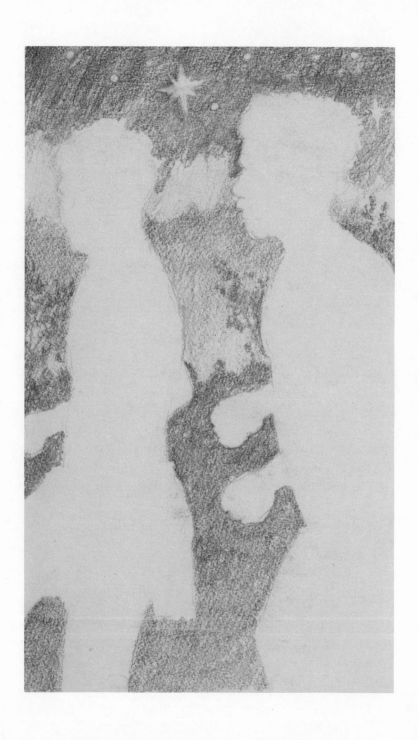

The Stellar Dance

~

Aboriginal Peoples of Australia

The Aboriginal peoples of Australia, like all hunters and gatherers, lived in small groups, altogether making up some seven hundred tribes. Each tribe travelled within an area of several hundred square miles, following the trails laid down by their mythic ancestor who left words and musical notes along with footprints. These song lines took them on well-worn paths to places where animals and plants were more plentiful.

Being on the move so often, the tribe had to travel light, carrying just the tools necessary to get food. The women needed sticks to gather seeds, roots, and fruits to fill their coolamons, wooden dishes. The men carried hunting weapons that included boomerang, spear, and woomera, a wooden spear thrower. They would hunt animals, such as kangaroo, emu, and flying fox, a large fruit-eating bat.

The Aboriginal peoples call the time of the world's creation the Dreamtime. This was when the spirit ancestors arose from the earth and took journeys through the empty countryside. They formed waterholes and rivers to sustain life. They populated the land with animals and plants. It was during the Dreamtime that the Great Spirit made humans.

~

Back in the Dreamtime, when the earth was young, the Great Spirit, Baiame, made his home in a mountain. Baiame looked out at what he had created. "The world is full of beauty," he said, "but it needs dancing life to fulfill its destiny."

With that, the Great Spirit created man. It was one of these very creations, a man named Priepriggie, who brought the Milky Way into being. This is how it happened.

In northeast Australia, in a narrow glen, lived a small tribe of valley people. Unlike other tribes in that area, they danced every night, not just on special occasions.

In the dark above, the stars were in chaos. They wheeled this way and that way, a turmoil of lights across the sky. Like a crackling fire shooting sparks in all directions, the stars glinted first here, then there. From one blink of the eye to the next, the night looked vastly different. No one could tell one part of the sky from another, for it was always changing. It seemed that the stars were tousled by fierce heavenly winds.

Unlike the chaos of the stars in the sky above, there was order in that dip of earth far below. Priepriggie brought harmony to his people with songs and chants and dances that flowed and pulsed in the night.

"Ah! Priepriggie," the people said. "Such a singer, such a hunter, such a medicine man. He is so gifted, so skilled, and so powerful, surely he can get the stars to move together and dance to his songs."

In order to have the strength to dance hour after hour, these men and women needed to find food enough for their one big meal. During the day, the women gathered plants and dug roots while the men hunted. And the one who always brought back the most food was Priepriggie.

One morning just at daybreak, Priepriggie began his hunting expedition in a different direction. This time he walked along the river bank, stepping softly through the low mist.

Coming to an enormous tree, he saw a multitude of flying fox hanging from the branches like bunches of berries. These flying fox were sleeping after their own nightly foray for food. These bats made delicious morsels, but Priepriggie needed more than that to feed his hungry tribe. He then spotted their leader, who was so gigantic that he alone would make a filling meal for all the people.

The enormous bat was asleep in the very center of the huddled multitude. With steps lighter than a spider's, Priepriggie circled the tree to close in on his target. He carefully placed his spear into his *woomera*. Bit by bit, he drew the *woomera* back to launch it. Priepriggie drove the *woomera* forward, sending the spear humming toward his target. The spear lanced the bat and transfixed him to the tree.

The thunderous blow awoke the throng of flying fox. They rushed up with the clicking of angry wings. Like a whirling dust devil, they flew round and round the tree, awaiting the flight of their leader.

But he did not join them. Only after going around and around did the circling band see that their leader would never come again; the spear which killed him was still quivering.

Then they spied the *woomera* on the ground. Squatting behind was Priepriggie, awaiting the moment when he could carry off his gigantic bounty. Down plunged the flying fox. They hovered around the hunter only for an instant. They swooped down on him so quickly, he could not escape.

Four flying fox grasped his hair in their claws.

Two drew up to his chin, each placing one wing underneath his jaw and extending the other. The others ringed themselves around Priepriggie. So equally spaced were they that one side of the hunter's body could have been a clear pool's reflection of the other. One bat was under his right jaw, one under his left. Each elbow was upheld by seven, his thigh had nine, his knee two. Several small bats were under his feet. Priepriggie was now cloaked in flying fox.

As if on signal, each bat began to beat its one free wing. They moved in concert, like one body, ascending higher and higher, lifting the hunter high above the clouds. Priepriggie vanished into the heavens beyond, far from sight.

As the sun went down that evening, his tribe gathered to eat and to dance, as they had done each night. They built a fire in the stone fire pit. But they had little to cook, for neither game nor roots filled their *coolamon*s. They were hoping that Priepriggie had a successful hunt, enough to feed them all, but he was nowhere to be seen.

"Where is he?" asked Loolo, a very fearful man. "This is not like Priepriggie. Something awful must have happened."

"Any one of us can have a little difficulty that slows us down, even Priepriggie," said Wahn, the oldest man of the tribe. "While we are waiting for him to return, let us dance and sing. It will help us forget our hunger. And maybe our songs will bring

Priepriggie back that much sooner."

The men and women tried to dance, but their legs were like fallen logs, as heavy as their hearts. They needed someone to set the rhythm, to lead them in their dance.

Suddenly, a singer's voice came from afar. They stopped and strained their ears.

"Do you hear that?" said Nungeena, a young woman with ears sharp as a spear. "That is Priepriggie's voice."

Louder and louder came the song, clearer and clearer was the rhythm. It came from high above them. They lifted their heads up, toward the source of the welcome sounds. They scanned the sky, looking for Priepriggie. But they did not see him.

Instead, they beheld the stars. The stars! No longer were they a turmoil of lights, scattered this way and that way. No longer were they like the sparks from their fire pit, glinting here and there. The stars were moving together, dancing to the rhythms of Priepriggie's music!

"We, too, will dance like the stars," said Wahn, starting to nod in time to the beat.

As if weights had been lifted from their hearts, they began to step lightly, sometimes in a line, sometimes in a circle. And with the dance steps, they sang to the music coming from above.

It was astonishing. Priepriggie was leading both the people and the stars in a new dance, one never done before. On and on they danced, far into the night.

The song ended, and with it, the dance. Exhausted, all the dancers dropped to the earth.

Wahn, Loolo, Nungeena, and, in fact, all the tribe collapsed to the ground. When they blinked open their eyes, their mouths dropped in awe.

The stars, too, had dropped, and were lying exactly where they had fallen after the festive dance. No longer were they scattered this way and that. No longer were they glinting here and there. Now the stars were arrayed across the sky, forming a band of light.

Priepriggie's stellar dance had taken the chaos of the starry heavens and made the Milky Way, the soft light that traverses the sky from one end to the other.

The people grieved for Priepriggie. They missed him, for it was he who had found the most nourishing food for their bodies. It was he who had offered the most refreshing food for the spirit. But they knew, as if Baiame, the Great Spirit himself, had told them, that only his song and dance could have enchanted the stars into harmony. Only Priepriggie could have led the stellar dance, the dance that gave all below the joy of the milky light that now stretches across the heavens.

A Raiment for Rangi

∾

Maori

A thousand years ago, a group of Polynesians took to their canoes. These amazingly talented navigators crossed several thousand miles of the Pacific Ocean to settle in New Zealand. The Maoris were tall, had black, wavy hair, and tattooed their skin with elaborate designs. They were skilled woodcarvers, farmers, seamen, and warriors. They knew how to hunt and gather in the fertile forests that covered their beautiful islands.

In Maori lore, the earliest being was Io, the causer of motion and space and moving earth; then came Rangi, the god of space, and Pahpah, the goddess of matter; and finally, their children. These young gods created the plants and animals on earth and the heavenly bodies in the sky.

∾

In the distant void, Io, the great causer of light and dark, of land and waters, of motion and space, dwelt alone. For a long while, it was so. Then, from himself, Io created two beings: Rangi and Pahpah.

Through the vastness of time, Rangi and Pahpah clung tightly to each other. In the darkness between them, eleven sons were born. These children were destined by Io to become great gods. From the time they were small, Io told each child what was preordained for him, so each knew what tasks he would have to perform to bring the world into being.

Dark eons passed. The growing children lived in the nooks and crannies between their parents. But they became more and more restless, more and more distressed that they were trapped in narrow spaces without light.

The young gods assembled in a dark pit and conferred. One after another, they spoke.

"Pahpah and Rangi are good parents. They love us and protect us, but we are no longer babies who must cling to them. We cannot carry out the tasks that Io has assigned us. We cannot call other beings into existence without light. We cannot create the world."

"There is only one way to gain our freedom, to fulfill our destiny," Tu-matuenga, the fiercest brother snarled. "We must slay our mother and father. Once they are gone, we will have light."

"No," answered Tane-mahuta, his more sensible brother. "It would be much better to simply separate them. Let Rangi be far above us! Let Pahpah be at our feet, our earth! True, we shall no longer be as close to Rangi, for he will be beyond our reach, but Pahpah will always be a caring mother to us."

"Agreed," said Rongo, the god of cultivated food. "I will try first." He put his hoe down next to the stunted kumara and taro plants. He pressed and struggled against both parents, but his efforts failed.

Tangaroa, the god of fish and reptiles, emerged from a small stream. "Let me try," he said. He butted his head against Rangi and Pahpah, but they stayed just where they'd been for the long years.

Then Rangi snapped, "Enough! Your jostling hurts! Stop it this instant!"

But the young gods kept pushing. They could not fulfill their destinies if they stayed trapped in the dark narrow spaces.

So, Haumia-tikitiki, the god of naturally growing food, parted the withered wild berries and stepped over the yellowing ferns to try his hand at letting in light. He, too, made absolutely no headway.

After that, Tu-matuenga, the god of fierce human beings, teeth bared and fists clenched, pummeled and kicked his parents. But he was as unsuccessful as his brothers. All his efforts brought only Rangi's angry rumbling.

At last, Tane-mahuta, god of forests, birds, and insects, began to shove with his hands and arms. That did nothing. Then, he stood with his head on his mother, Pahpah, and his feet against his father, Rangi. He strained and pressed, heaving his back and pushing all the harder.

Because Io had made Tane-mahuta the promoter of all life, he had created him much stronger than his brothers. Drawing upon that extra power, Tane thrust once more with all his might.

Miraculously, Rangi and Pahpah were parted, one from the other. They both groaned and cried out, "Why do you rend us apart?"

"Ah," Tane answered, "Io always told us we were born to do very special jobs. But we cannot, for there has been only darkness. All creatures—birds and insects, fish and reptiles, human beings—must have light and space, to live and grow and to have young. That is why we *must* part you. Only when you are parted and light enters can the world come into being."

Tane did not stop there. He kept pushing. Straining, he pressed them farther and farther apart, separating them forever, creating Mother Earth and Father Sky.

Suddenly, the light that Io had caused to shine so long ago broke through the nooks and crannies that trapped the brothers. The young gods spread their arms, glorying in this wash of brightness. As they breathed the air of freedom, they envisioned their new world. They saw the beauty to come: streams teeming with fish, lush fields of green, forests with succulent roots and berries, animals making snug homes.

With this vision, they each began their tasks. Tane planted trees, to make homes for the birds and insects, his children. Then humans came to Tane's garden and dwelled there.

Tane was delighted with the way plants and animals lived on Mother Earth. Indeed, her rolling hills were covered with rich green forests. Her dipping valleys were bright with burgeoning flowers. Colorful birds darted here and there, filling the air with song.

In the morning light, the moist earth glistened. Tane realized that these sparkling drops of dew were actually Father Sky's falling tears, his continuing sorrow at being parted from Mother Earth.

Tane looked again at beautiful Mother Earth. Then he lifted his eyes up and saw how cold and gray and sad Father Sky was. Tane took pity upon him. It was time to give him beauty too, a special kind of splendor. Taking the sun, Tane placed it behind Rangi, so that it would move across the heavens during the day. The bright sunshine illuminated the sky, giving it a perfect brilliance.

When night fell, he put the moon in front of Rangi. *That is good,* thought Tane, *but not quite good enough.* Tane said to his father, "When it is day, O Rangi, you are a lovely sight to behold. At night, though, until the moon comes out, all is dark and sad. You need something more. I will seek the raiment that you deserve."

Tane searched each corner of the sky to find attire befitting Rangi. A glowing red cape caught his eye. With a sweep of his arms, he spread the cape in all directions. He stepped back to look at it, but shook his head. Lovely as it was, it was not quite worthy of his father. He flung the cape aside, leaving just a strip of glowing red at the horizon which we can see at the time of the setting sun.

Tane went from one end of the world to the

other, searching for the perfect raiment. At last he knew what would be exactly right. He made a huge dark mantle, which he compressed into a small bundle and laid at the edge of the horizon. Then he travelled to Maunga-nui, the Great Mountain, where his brother Ruaumoko, the god of earthquakes and volcanoes, lived. Ruaumoko had many, many children—the Shining Ones—who came forth from volcanoes as fiery nuggets.

Tane told Ruaumoko of his plan: he would fasten some of the Shining Ones to a dark mantle for Father Sky. The volcano god immediately went to the hot bed of lava and gathered many of his children. He and Tane cast these glowing oval nuggets into an elongated basket.

Taking the basket of precious lights, Tane departed for the far horizon to gather the mantle. Then he sped to Rangi. Tane unwrapped the raiment and cast the soft mantle of darkness over his father. He reached into the basket and placed some of the Shining Ones here and there on the robe. Right in the middle, he stretched the sparkling basket. Tane carefully attached the basket to the raiment, so that the mass of twinkling lights would curve completely across Father Sky.

Tane stepped back to get a good look at the cloak. He saw that Rangi's full splendor was revealed. All was as it should be.

Now, when the sun goes down to rest, Rangi

shakes out his mantle till the heavens are filled with his beauty and the lights of the Shining Ones. And at the center of his radiant raiment, the long, star-filled basket reaches from one end of the robe to the other, giving it that soft sweep of light that is the Milky Way.

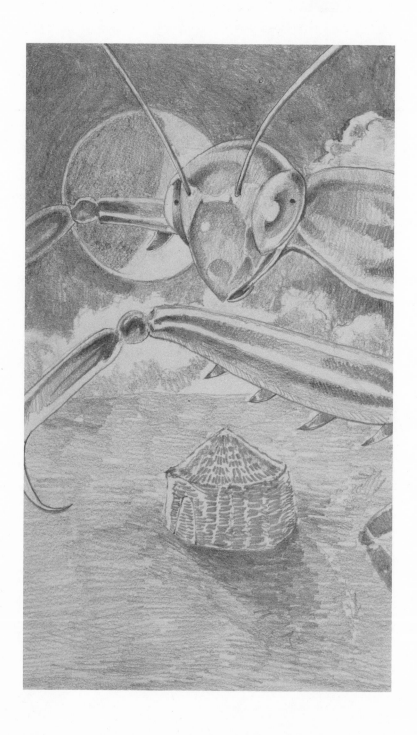

The Girl Who Threw Wood Ashes into the Sky

~

The San of the Kalahari

The San people (whom the Europeans called Bushmen) have lived for eons in the Kalahari desert. Short in stature, they speak Khoisan, a most unusual language that incorporates clicks made with the tongue and mouth.

Living in the desert in small groups, San know every inch of the hundreds of square miles they roam. They know where the lion and lynx prowl and where the gemsbok and springbok graze. They know and can imitate the call of every bird and animal. They recognize which dried tendrils have roots succulent enough to give them much-needed moisture. They know how to poison the tips of their hunting arrows with a paste ground from special plants and grubs.

They respect and depend on all of nature, for everything is related. Indeed, these people think of the sun, moon, and stars as members of their family, beloved ones that they can hear, speak to, and almost touch. The heavenly bodies and everything else in the San world were brought into being by !kaggen. This San creator takes the form of a praying mantis, an insect they consider sacred.

San girls, like girls in many other tribes, are initiated into adulthood by being isolated when they first menstruate. They are not allowed to return to the tribe until their period is over. Having never been completely alone for so long, many girls find it a terrifying experience.

~

In the time of the people of the early race, when the half moon was in the sky, a girl, whose name shall not be uttered, was on the verge of becoming a woman.

On that late afternoon, her mother took her by the hand. She led her daughter away from their small village. Through the tall, rustling grasses they trod, paying little attention to a spotted hyena loping across the veld. They passed the rocks covered with chattering baboons, "the people who sit on their heels." They crossed the path of a porcupine lumbering off toward its tunnel. On and on they walked, until they came to a small hut the mother had made of reed mats.

"Because your body is changing, you will have to be in this hut alone. You must stay here by yourself until you are altogether a woman," the mother said. "Only when you have become fully a woman may you leave. Only then may you lift your eyes and look afar. Only then may you walk about like all women. When the moon is full, you will be altogether a woman. Then I will come for you. Till that time, you must stay alone in this hut."

The girl listened, becoming more and more scared and unhappy. She put her head down, her eyes filling with tears, but said nothing.

As the sun left the sky, the mother ordered her into the hut and closed the tiny opening. The girl heard the quiet footsteps fade away. She was now completely alone. Only a small wood fire lit the dark hut.

She thought about how long it would be until she would hear her mother's steps again. It was now the time of the half moon. Every day, she knew, the moon's belly would swell more and more. It would take seven days until the moon would be full.

As the girl sat in her misery, she suddenly thought of how the moon came to be on high. She remembered how *!kaggen,* the divine Mantis, had wanted some light in the night sky.

!kaggen *took off one of his shoes and said to it, "I will call you `Moon,' the light who walks in the night. You will be altogether the moon. You will walk across* *the night sky, as a shoe does across the bush."*

With that, the Praying Mantis cast the shoe up, into the darkness. That shoe became altogether the Moon. The beautiful, bright moon walks in the night, feeling that he is a shoe.

The girl thought about the moon with his changing belly. She pushed the door ajar and saw the half moon shining.

As she looked at him, she knew that if she had a special light, she would not feel so totally alone.

"Why I, too, could be like *!kaggen* the Mantis," she said. "I shall give the night sky another kind of light."

In the dim light of the moon, she searched the ground near the hut for special roots. With a sharpened stick she dug one and held it to her nose. The odor told her it was exactly what she wanted. She dug many of these woody roots and carried them back to the tiny hut, where she threw them upon the fire.

The roots burned down, giving the air a perfumed scent. Gray ashes fell away from the glowing coals. She took a handful of these cool wood ashes from the fire.

She looked down at them and spoke. "I will call you *!kô*, the Milky Way. You which are wood ashes here must altogether become the Milky Way. You must lie glowing while the stars sail along outside you. You must radiate white along the sky,

!kô, to guide travellers through the darkness."

With that, the girl swept her arm upwards, hurling the wood ashes up, up into the deep darkness. The ashes scattered on high. And the wood ashes altogether became *!kô,* the Milky Way.

The stars sail on and then fetch the daybreak. Still, the Milky Way lies nicely across the sky, reaching all the way to the place from which the girl had strewn the wood ashes. As the Sun comes out, the Milky Way pales.

But when darkness comes again, when the stars sail brightly along, the Milky Way glows across the sky. *!kô* guides all who travel by night back to their own homes, to the warmth of their own fires.

Nagaik, the Path to
the Place of Abundance

∽

Toba Indians of the Gran Chaco
in Argentina

The Toba Indians were a proud, warlike people who wore cloaks of animal skin, ornaments of feathers and shells, and, in their earlobes, wooden plugs. Living in bands of fifty to a hundred in the Chaco bush of northeast Argentina, they hunted rhea, deer, peccary, and jaguar, smoked fish, collected wild fruits and tubers, and grew squash, corn, and melons.

Like other hunter-gatherers, they could never be sure of finding enough food. Some days they feasted. Other times famine prevailed, with so little to eat that only the gnawing pain of hunger filled their bellies.

It is no wonder that, for the Tobas, the Milky Way was a road certain to lead to a land with more than enough for everyone.

∽

It was summer, the time when Sun was a heavy, old woman, who took much time plodding across the sky. Her tortoise-like steps stretched the days, making nights come late.

One morning, Sun had walked only partway up from the east when her light shone upon a chiñiñi bird, a sandpiper. With his tiny beak, he was weaving tendrils to strengthen the unsteady tree that bridged the deep ravine at the edge of the bush.

He heard a chattering group of girls in the distance. No doubt, he thought, they are out looking for food. Chiñiñi knew they must be hungry, for there had been little to eat on this side of the canyon.

The small sandpiper listened to the girls as he

wove the tendrils in and out.

"We've combed the bush, ever since Sun started her walk early this morning, and found nothing but a withered root," one girl said. "Let us stop under this palm and plan where to go next."

Chiñiñi saw another girl walk from the palm tree to the edge of the canyon. He saw her delight as she looked across the split in the earth to the other side where many trees were growing, ripe with fruit—chanar and mistol and sweet carob. He knew that her empty stomach must be growling loudly.

She ran back to her friends. "Come!" she shouted. "Wonderful food. We just have to find a way to the other side, to cross the abyss."

The girls leapt up and ran to the edge. They looked across at the luscious fruit bending the branches of the trees. The girls trod along the side, searching for long vines to swing across, searching for any way to reach that land of plenty.

Then Chiñiñi saw the girls turn and come back toward him, toward the tree that was lying across the deep narrow abyss. The slightest whisper of a wind blew along the canyon walls. The tree creaked as it swayed to and fro. Despite its notched grooves and palm frond railing, the bird knew the bridge was not safe to use.

But when the girls reached the tree spanning the abyss, they could not contain their eagerness.

"Here," they called to one another. "Here we

can cross. Soon we'll have all we want to eat."

"No," said Chiñiñi, desperately trying to block their way. "Don't step on the bridge yet. I haven't finished my repairs."

But the girls paid him no attention. Their eyes were fixed on the fruit across the chasm. They certainly would not wait. One after the other, they brushed by the tiny bird, stepped onto the tree, and started to cross.

In the blink of an eye, the soft creak became an ear-splitting crack, and the tree gave way under their weight. The girls reached for the fronds, but their stretched hands felt nothing but air. They plunged down, down into the depths.

Chiñiñi gasped. He leaned over the edge, but could see nothing. He looked to where the bridge had been and shook his head sadly.

Slowly, he turned away, toward the wild undergrowth.

Just at that moment, a jabiru stork stepped out of the brush.

"Where are you coming from?" asked Chiñiñi.

"From a faraway place, where there is little food," answered Jabiru.

"And where are you going?"

"To the village of the people who live yonder," Jabiru pointed with his beak. "But why is there nothing to take creatures across here?"

"Ah! There was a bridge, but it broke under too much weight," Chiñiñi replied. "And I don't have the tools to make a new one. But you look like a skillful creature. Surely, with your keen-edged bill, you can build another."

"Yes," answered Jabiru. "I can do that. You will see my skill in building a new bridge."

No sooner had he spoken than Jabiru began to fell tall trees. With his hard, sharp beak, he cut them into long boards.

Carefully, he laid the planks across the chasm. Then he took a palm tree and placed it along one side to steady those who crossed.

Sun was now in the west, walking slowly toward the night.

"Come, Chiñiñi," Jabiru said. "Let us try the bridge."

The sandpiper joined the stork and the two birds walked on the newly finished span.

"You have done well, Jabiru," said Chiñiñi, admiring the stork's handiwork.

"Now," the sharp-beaked bird said, "I shall make a wide path that leads to the bridge. This will be a well-marked path, one that no creature can miss."

Just as Sun took her last steps in the sky, Jabiru set fire to the bush. He did not create a small flame, but one that burned a large track. So thick and broad was the path that it is still full of white smoke and ashes, even today.

Before Chiñiñi's eyes, the smoke and ashes were transformed into a wash of glittering white lights on high. It became that bright path in the sky, Nagaik, that leads those who are hungry to a land of plenty.

And on the clearest of starry nights, the wind carries the whisper of the girls from the depths of the canyon. *Follow Nagaik,* it says. *This path, the Milky Way, will take you to the splendid feast awaiting you on the other side of the heavens.*

Notes

THE SEVENTH NIGHT OF THE SEVENTH MOON
This story was adapted from Lafcadio Hearn's *The Romance of the Milky Way and Other Studies and Stories.* Variations of this tale appear in Gertrude Jobes' *Dictionary of Mythology, Folklore and Symbols;* E.C. Krupp's *Beyond the Blue Horizon: Myths and Legends of the Sun, Moon, Stars, and Planets;* and in *Funk and Wagnall's Dictionary of Folklore and Legend,* edited by Maria Leach. Jeanne Lee retells a Chinese version in *Legend of the Milky Way.*

THE MILK THAT FLEW ACROSS THE SKY
This story was adapted from Robert Graves' *The Greek Myths.* An account of the tale also appears in Jacob Grimm's *Teutonic Mythology,* in Jobes' two books, *Dictionary of Mythology, Folklore and Symbols* and *Outer Space: Myths, Names, Meanings, and Calendars;* and in Krupp's *Beyond the Blue Horizon.*

YIKÁÍSDÁHÍ, WHICH AWAITS THE DAWN
This story was adapted from Father Berard Haile's *Starlore among the Navaho.* This Navajo tale also appears in Trudy Griffin-Pierce's *Earth Is My Mother, Sky Is My Father;* in Jean Monroe and Ray Williamson's *They Dance in the Sky;* and in Margaret Link's *The Pollen Path: A Collection of Navajo Myths.*

THE STELLAR DANCE
This story was adapted from A.W. Reed's *Aboriginal Stories of Australia,* from Alan Marshall's *People of the Dreamtime,* and from Roslynn Haynes, "Dreaming the Sky," *Sky and Telescope,* September 1997.

A RAIMENT FOR RANGI

This story was adapted from A.W. Reed's *Myths and Legends of Maoriland;* James Cowan's *Legends of the Maori;* Antony Alpers' *Maori Myths and Legends;* W. Dittmer's *Te tohunga: The Ancient Legends and Traditions of the Maoris;* and Johannes Andersen's *Myths and Legends of the Polynesians.*

THE GIRL WHO THREW WOOD ASHES INTO THE SKY

This story was adapted from Bleek and Lloyd's *Specimens of Bushmen Folklore.* The two authors and Bleek's daughter studied the language in the late 1800s and translated stories from several Bushmen storytellers. This tale also appears in Penny Miller's *Myths and Legends of Southern Africa;* Jobes' *Outer Space: Myths, Names, Meanings, and Calendars;* and Krupp's *Beyond the Blue Horizon.*

NAGAIK, THE PATH TO THE PLACE OF ABUNDANCE

This story is adapted from Johannes Wilbert and Karin Simoneau's *Folk Literature of the Toba Indians* and Alfred Metraux's *Myths of the Toba and Pilaga Indians of the Gran Chaco.* The tale also is referred to in *Funk and Wagnall's Dictionary of Folklore and Legend.*

★

Glossary

Alcmene — *(alk-mee′ ne)* Greek.
Queen of Thebes, wife of Amphitryon, mother of Heracles and Iphicles.

Amphitryon — *(am-fit′ ri- on)* Greek.
King of Thebes.

Athena — *(a- thee′ na)* Greek.
Goddess of wisdom, Zeus's daughter who sprang forth from her father's head.

Baiame — *(Bye-am-eh′)* Australian Aborigine.
The Great Spirit who created the world.

Chiñiñi — *(chee-nyee-nyee)* Toba Indian.
A sandpiper.

coolamon — *(koo′luh-mun)* Australian Aborigine.
A basin made of wood or bark for carrying food.

Dilyehe — *(till′ yeh-heh)* Navajo.
Circlet of stars also known as the Pleiades.

Diné — *(tih′ neh)* Navajo.
The term Navajos call themselves.

galaxias kyklos — *(gal-a-ksee′ ahs kee′ klose)* Greek.
This means "milky circle" which was what the ancient Greeks called the Milky Way.

Hastyésini — *(hahss-tee-ess-ee-nee)* Navajo.
The Fire God.

Haumia-tikitiki — *(how′ mih-uh-tih-kih-tih-kih)* Maori.
The god of naturally growing food.

Hera — *(hair′ a)* Greek.
Queen of the heavens and wife of Zeus.

Heracles — *(hair'a kleez)* Greek.
Zeus' son and great hero who performed incredible feats.

Hikoboshi — *(hick' oh' bah' shih)* Japanese.
The heavenly herdsman.

Iphicles — *(if'-i-kleez)* Greek.
Twin brother of Heracles.

Io — *(ih'-oh)* Maori.
The causer of motion and space and moving earth.

Jabiru — *(yah-bee-roo)* Toba Indian.
A stork.

!kaggen — San.
The creator who takes the form of a praying mantis.

!kô — San.
The Milky Way.

In the Khoisan language, the sound pictured by a "!" is a special kind of click. This click is made by curling the tip of the tongue against the roof of the mouth and pulling it down suddenly, with a lot of force.

Kalahari — *(kah'-le-har-ee)*
The great desert in southern Africa.

Kami — *(kah'-mih')* Japanese.
A heavenly deity.

Maunga-nui — *(mah'-ung-ah-noo-ih)* Maori.
The Great Mountain.

Medusa — *(muh-doo'-sa)* Greek.
In Greek mythology, Medusa was a Gorgon, a monster with clawed serpents for hair and eyes that turned men to stone in one glance. She was killed by the hero Perseus.

Nagaik — *(nah-ga-eek)* Toba Indian.
The path that leads to the land of plenty, the Milky Way.

Nungeena — *(nung-ee-nah')* Australian Aborigine.
A woman of the tribe.

Pahpah — *(puh'-puh)* Maori.
The goddess of matter and earth.

Perseus — *(pur'-see-us)* Greek.
The Greek hero, king of Argos and Tiryns, who killed
Medusa.

Priepriggie — *(pree-preeg-ghee')* Australian Aborigine.
The leader of a small tribe in Northeast Australia.

Rangi — *(rung'-ih)* Maori.
The god of space and heavens.

Rongo — *(rawng'-aw)* Maori.
The god of cultivated food.

Ruaumoko — *(ruh-ow'-maw-kaw)* Maori.
The god of earthquakes and volcanoes.

Tanabata — *(tah'-nah'-bah'-ta')* Japanese.
The weaving lady of the heavens.

Tane-mahuta — *(tun'-eh-muh-hoo-tuh)* Maori.
The god of forests, birds, and insects. Promoter of all life.

Tangaroa — *(tung'-uh-raw-uh)* Maori.
God of fish and reptiles.

Tien Ho — *(tee-en' hoe)* Chinese.
The Celestial River, which is also called the Milky Way.

Tu-matuenga — *(too-muh-too-eng'-uh)* Maori.
God of fierce human beings.

woomera — *(wum-er-ah)* Australian Aborigine.
A wooden spear thrower.

Yikáísdáhí — *(yik-ice-dah-hi)* Navajo.
The Navajo name for the Milky Way, meaning "which
awaits the dawn."

Zeus — *(zooss')* Greek.
Most powerful of the Greek gods, ruler of heaven and earth, husband of Hera and father of Heracles.

Bibliography

Alpers, Antony. *Maori Myths & Tribal Legends*. London: J. Murray, 1964.

Andersen, Johannes C. *Myths & Legends of the Polynesians*. Tokyo: Charles E. Tuttle, 1969.

Baglin, Douglass, & David R. Moore. *People of the Dreamtime; the Australian Aborigines*. New York & Tokyo: John Weatherill, 1970.

Blake, John. *Astronomical Myths*. London: Macmillan, 1877.

Bleek, W.H.I., and L.C. Lloyd. *Specimens of Bushman Folklore*. London: George Allen, 1911.

Bruchac, Joseph. *The Story of the Milky Way*. New York: Dial, 1995.

Dittmers, W. *Te Tohunga: The Ancient Legends & Traditions of the Maoris*. Papakura, New Zealand: Southern Reprints, 1989.

Gifford, Douglas. *Warriors, Gods, and Spirits from Central and South American Mythology*. New York: Peter Bedrick, 1983.

Graves, Robert. *The Greek Myths*. Harmondsworth, Middlesex, England: Penguin Books, 1955.

Green, Jacob. *Astronomical Recreations: or Sketches of the Relative Positions and Mythological History of the Constellations*. Philadelphia: Anthony Finley, 1824.

Griffin-Pierce, Trudy. *Earth Is My Mother, Sky Is My Father*. Albuquerque: University of New Mexico Press, 1992.

Grimm, Jacob. *Teutonic Mythology*. 1883. Reprint, New York: Dover Press, 1966.

Haile, Berard. *Starlore among the Navaho*. Santa Fe: Museum of Navajo Ceremonial Art, 1947.

Haynes, Roslynn. "Dreaming the Sky," *Sky & Telescope,* v. 94 # 3, p 72-75 September 1997.

Hearn, Lafcadio. *The Romance of the Milky Way and Other Studies and Stories.* Boston: Houghton Mifflin, 1905.

Jobes, Gertrude. *Dictionary of Mythology, Folklore and Symbols.* New York: Scarecrow Press, 1961.

Jobes, Gertrude, and James Jobes. *Myths: Names, Meanings, & Calendars.* New York: Scarecrow Press, 1964.

Krupp, E.C. *Beyond the Blue Horizon: Myths and Legends of the Sun, Moon, Stars, and Planets.* New York: HarperCollins, 1991.

Leach, Maria. *The Beginning: Creation Myths around the World.* New York: Funk & Wagnalls, 1956.

———, ed. *Funk & Wagnalls Dictionary of Folklore and Legend.* New York: Funk & Wagnalls, 1950.

Lee, Jeanne M. *Legend of the Milky Way.* New York: Henry Holt, 1982.

Link, Margaret Schevill. *The Pollen Path: A Collection of Navajo Myth.* Stanford: Stanford University Press, 1956.

Luomala, Kaharine. *Maui-of-a Thousand Tricks: His Oceanic and European Biographers.* Honolulu: Bernice P. Bishop Museum Bulletin 198, 1949.

Marshall, Alan, *People of the Dreamtime.* Melbourne: Cheshire Pty, Ltd., 1952.

McCulloch, Canon John Arnott, ed. *The Mythology of All Races.* Boston: Archaeological Institute of America, 1932.

Metraux, Alfred. *Myths of the Toba and Pilaga Indians of the Gran Chaco.* Philadelphia: American Folklore Society, 1946.

Miller, Penny. *Myths & Legends of Southern Africa.* Capetown: T. V. Bulpin, 1979.

Monroe, Jean Guard, and Ray A. Williamson. *They Dance in the Sky: Native American Star Myths.* Boston: Houghton Mifflin, 1987.

Reed, A.W. *Aboriginal Stories of Australia.* Frenchs Forest, New South Wales, Australia: Reed Books, 1980.

————. *Myths and Legends of Maoriland*. London: George Allen & Unwin, 1946.

Scott, Oral E. *The Stars in Myth and Fact*. Caldwell, Idaho: Caxton Printers, 1942.

Vautier, Ghislaine. *The Way of the Stars: Greek Legends of the Constellations*. Cambridge: Cambridge University Press, 1982.

Whyte, Charles. *The Constellations and their History*. London: Charles Griffin, 1928.

Wilbert, Johannes, and Karin Simoneau. *Folk Literature of the Toba Indians*. Los Angeles: UCLA Latin American Center Publications, 1982.

Williamson, Ray A., and Claire R. Farrer. *Earth and Sky: Visions of the Cosmos in Native American Folklore*. Albuquerque: University of New Mexico Press, 1992.

Acknowledgments

The Celestial River grew from a story told by my sister-in-law, Judit Stenn. On a dark summer night, in an alpine valley high in the Rockies, we were gazing at the resplendent stream of light that stretched across the sky. Suddenly, Judit remembered a story from her Hungarian childhood about the Milky Way. That tale, for which I am so grateful, led me to a host of others from all over the world.

I am most grateful, also, to my writers' group: Beverly Gherman, Maxine Schur, Gabrielle Rilleau, and Shirleyann Costigan, for all their encouragement, criticism, and friendship.

And to Lubert.

ATHENS REGIONAL LIBRARY SYSTEM

Discard 7/99

3 3207 00552 7001

ARL-DOC
BOGART BRANCH LIBRARY
C/O ATHENS REGIONAL LIBRARY
2025 BAXTER STREET
ATH

WITHDRAWN